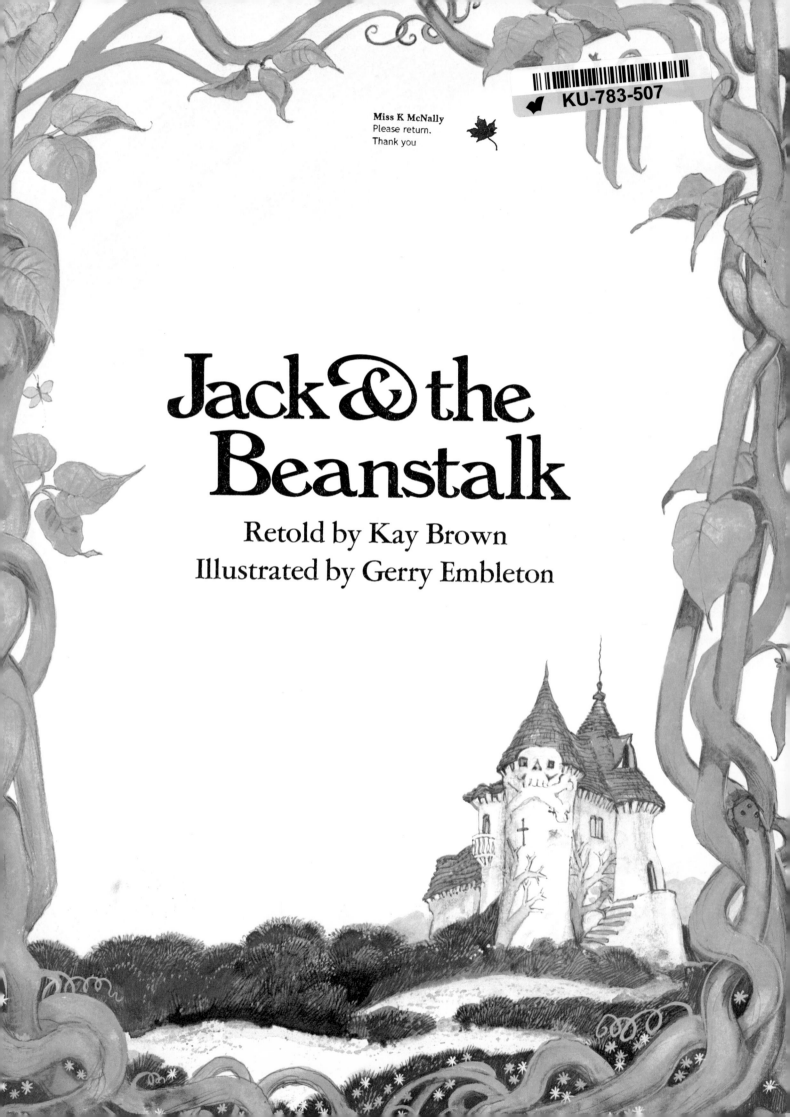

Jack & the Beanstalk

Retold by Kay Brown

Illustrated by Gerry Embleton

Our story is about a boy called Jack. He lived with his mother in a tiny, old cottage; Jack's father had died some years before. The cottage was badly in need of repair: when it rained the roof let in water, the small garden was overgrown with weeds and most of the fences had fallen down.

Jack and his mother kept a cow, Buttercup, whose milk they sold to buy food and material for their simple clothes. One day, however, Buttercup gave no milk and Jack's mother was very worried. 'What shall we do?' she asked Jack 'We have so little money saved and you are too young to get a job.'

Jack tried to cheer his mother but, when Buttercup gave no milk the next day, nor the next, he too began to worry. For a while they lived on their savings, but very soon the money was gone.

Very sadly Jack and his mother agreed the only thing they could do was to sell Buttercup. But as they were both very fond of the cow, it wasn't until they hadn't eaten for several days that Jack offered to take Buttercup to the market in town the next morning.

Jack was up early next day, hoping to leave with Buttercup before his mother was awake. However, she ran to the door with tears in her eyes, saying 'Be sure to get a good price for her: there are many rogues in town who may try to cheat you. And come straight home as soon as you have the money in your pocket.'

Jack said he would, kissed his mother (bravely trying to hide his own tears) and set off with Buttercup.

When Jack and Buttercup reached the town, the market square was crowded with people buying and selling, but no-one seemed interested in Buttercup. Jack was thinking about what he could say to his mother if he had to take Buttercup home again, when an old man with a long beard and kind face spoke to him. 'You look a bright sort of lad, Jack: how many beans make five?' Jack wondered how the stranger knew his name, but he answered quickly 'Two in each hand and one in your

mouth.' 'Quite right' said the man 'And here they are.' He pulled from his pocket a bag of strange looking beans. 'As you're such a clever chap. I don't mind doing a swap with you – your cow for these beans.' Jack didn't think much of this, but the old man told him 'These are no ordinary beans, my boy: if you plant them tonight, by tomorrow they'll have grown up to the sky. If I'm not right, you may have your cow back.' This seemed fair enough to Jack, who handed Buttercup to the stranger and put the beans safely in his pocket.

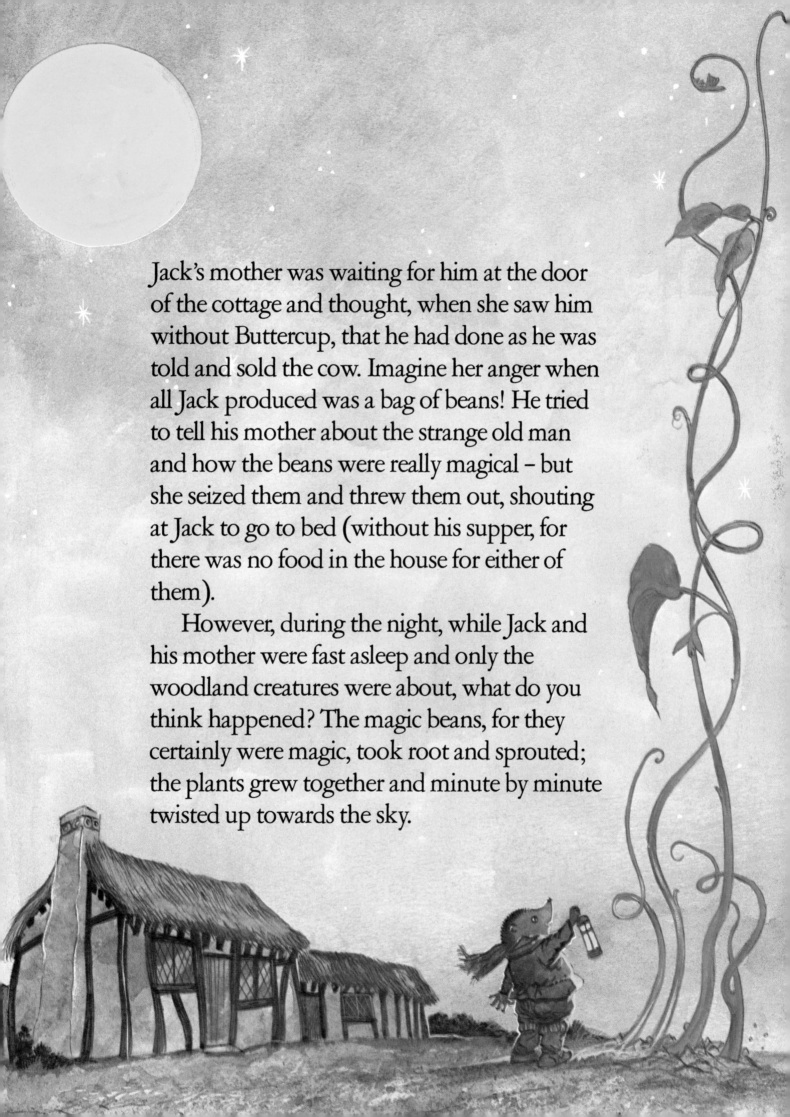

Jack's mother was waiting for him at the door of the cottage and thought, when she saw him without Buttercup, that he had done as he was told and sold the cow. Imagine her anger when all Jack produced was a bag of beans! He tried to tell his mother about the strange old man and how the beans were really magical – but she seized them and threw them out, shouting at Jack to go to bed (without his supper, for there was no food in the house for either of them).

However, during the night, while Jack and his mother were fast asleep and only the woodland creatures were about, what do you think happened? The magic beans, for they certainly were magic, took root and sprouted; the plants grew together and minute by minute twisted up towards the sky.

Next morning Jack awoke to find his bedroom in shadow although the sun was shining outside. He went to the window . . . there, twisting up and up right into the clouds, was the most enormous beanstalk! Jack was so excited he dressed quickly and woke his mother, who had quite forgotten to be cross with him. They both went into the garden to stare at the magic beanstalk: its stems were as big as a man's waist and its leaves like umbrellas.

Now, as you know, Jack was a brave boy and he loved an adventure. 'Mother, I must climb up and see what is at the top' he said. Jack's mother thought this was a dangerous idea but, after much persuasion and because Jack promised to be careful, she agreed to let him go.

He climbed and climbed and climbed until his legs ached; the thick, twisting stems became gradually thinner and then, quite suddenly, Jack was above the clouds and at the very top of the beanstalk.
He clambered off onto a grassy bank and looked around. The air was very still and quiet and Jack saw, not far away, a mysterious castle.

Jack realised how hungry he was (remember, he had had no supper or breakfast) and, being a brave sort of boy, decided to ask at the castle for food and a drink. When he reached the castle door, however, he realised that it was five times larger than any ordinary door; still, he knocked and waited. When it opened a great big woman peered down at him. Jack politely asked if she could spare him some breakfast. 'My man is an ogre and likes boys on toast better than anything' she told him 'but if you're really hungry you can take a chance. Come in and I'll find you something to eat.'

She led Jack to a huge kitchen where everything was so enormous it made Jack feel as small as a rabbit; the giantess busied herself preparing a boat-sized plate of bacon and eggs. Jack had only taken a few mouthfuls, however, when suddenly the castle shook and he heard a sound like thunder coming nearer and nearer. 'Quick' said the giant's wife to Jack 'He's coming! Hop into this cupboard and don't make a sound!' She just had time to close the cupboard doors when in crashed the giant: he sniffed the air for a moment and roared –

'Fee fi fo fum
I smell the blood of an Englishman
Be he alive or be he dead
I'll grind his bones to make my bread.'
'Nonsense, dear' said his wife soothingly 'You're imagining things.
Sit down now and I'll finish cooking your breakfast.' Jack, feeling
very uncomfortable in the cupboard, watched through a crack while
the giant ate three dozen eggs and a pile of bacon. He was even bigger
than Jack had imagined him to be: the sound of his eating was like a
distant earthquake and when he drank from his huge cup there was a
noise like streams rushing down a mountainside. 'I shouldn't make
him much of a meal' thought Jack, and felt a little less afraid.

When the giant had finished his breakfast he called 'Wife, bring
me the hen that lays the golden eggs.' The giantess returned with a
plain, brown hen which she set down on the table. 'Lay' boomed the
giant, and the hen laid an egg – a golden egg! The giant seemed
amused and again roared 'Lay' and once more the hen laid an egg of
solid gold. Jack, watching from the cupboard, could scarcely believe
his eyes as the hen laid golden eggs, one after another, at the
giant's command.

After a while the giant began to grow sleepy: he stretched his great legs and closed his eyes. Soon his snores were shaking the kitchen. Jack had, of course, been waiting for just such a chance to escape, but as he was climbing quietly down from the cupboard he realised the magic hen was still on the giant's table.

With his heart thumping Jack climbed onto the table, seized the

startled hen and tucked her under his arm. The hen squawked and
Jack felt sure the giant would wake up, but the thunderous
snores continued.

As fast as he could, Jack ran from the kitchen, hoping he could
remember the way along the tall corridors to the huge front door.
He didn't stop running until he reached the top of the beanstalk.

It was much easier climbing down the beanstalk and Jack was soon back safely in his own garden. His mother was overjoyed to see him and listened while Jack told of his adventure in the giant's castle. When he showed her the plain brown hen his mother didn't believe that such an ordinary looking bird could possibly lay anything other than ordinary eggs. 'Come, I'll show you' said Jack merrily. He put the hen on their table and ordered 'Lay.' Immediately there, shining and yellow, was an egg of solid gold! 'What did I tell you' Jack said to his mother 'Those beans were magical after all.'

Jack and his mother were poor no longer! They repaired the cottage roof, mended the fences and bought new furniture. There were new clothes, a good supply of firewood and a larder full of food – and Jack went back to the market to buy *two* cows so that they would always have plenty of milk.

But after a while Jack began to wonder what was going on at the top of the beanstalk and one morning, very early, he dressed and left the house. Once again, he climbed and climbed until his legs ached: at the top of the beanstalk above the clouds he saw the giant's castle. As before, he knocked boldly on the huge door; when the giantess opened it Jack again asked her for some food and drink. 'Haven't I seen you before?' she asked him. 'Weren't you here the day my husband lost the hen that laid the golden eggs?' 'I could tell you about that' said Jack 'but at the moment I'm too hungry to talk.' So the giant's wife led him into the enormous kitchen once more. She was about to cook some kippers for Jack when they heard a sound like mountains moving. 'Quick' said the giantess 'Into the oven with you.'

The rumbling came nearer and nearer and the castle began
to shake. Mighty footsteps echoed throughout the stone
passageway from the door. Jack knew that the giant would
be upon him in no time and he began to feel very small
and afraid.

Jack just had time to hide himself before the giant thundered into the room. 'Fee fi fo fum, I smell the blood of an Englishman' he roared. 'Nonsense' said his wife 'but I have two barrels full of kippers for your breakfast. Sit and eat!' So the giant ate his kippers and Jack's, too! When he had finished he told his wife to fetch the golden harp and placing it on the table he ordered 'Sing.' Immediately the harp began to sing a beautiful song, then another and another. Soon the giant fell asleep and his snores were like waves crashing on the rocks. Jack, seeing his chance to escape, ran from the oven: as he passed the table he reached up and grabbed the golden harp, but as he did so the harp gave a loud scream and shouted 'Master, Master!'

The giant awoke just in time to see
Jack disappearing with the harp. He
thundered along the corridors after Jack,
roaring and bellowing, but fast as he ran
Jack ran faster. Jack could see the tip of
the beanstalk in the distance and he
raced across the fields with the giant
close behind and the harp still
screaming under his arm. Jack had only
climbed down a few yards when the
beanstalk began to shake . . . the giant
was climbing down too!

Jack slithered and slid as fast as he could. He could hear the giant above him, snapping off branches as he clambered down furiously after Jack and the stolen harp.

As soon as Jack reached the ground he ran into the cottage. 'Mother quick, an axe!' he called breathlessly. 'The giant is almost here!'

Jack swung at the beanstalk with all his strength, just as the giant's great feet came into sight.

For a moment it seemed as though Jack was too late. Then, with a sound as though the earth was cracking open, the beanstalk swayed and crashed to the ground. There, tangled in its stems, lay the giant . . . dead!

Later, Jack told his mother all that had happened on his second visit to the giant's castle and showed her the magic harp. 'Sing' he commanded as the giant had done and, once more, the harp sang a strange and beautiful song. Jack's mother was so pleased to have her son safely home (and the beanstalk gone from the sky outside!) that she listened to his adventures again and again.